WELLINGTON'S BIG DAY OUT

STEVE SMALL

A Paula Wiseman Book
Simon & Schuster Books for Young Readers
New York   London   Toronto   Sydney   New Delhi

For Dad

SIMON & SCHUSTER BOOKS FOR YOUNG READERS
An imprint of Simon & Schuster Children's Publishing Division
1230 Avenue of the Americas, New York, New York 10020
© 2022 by Steve Small
First published in Great Britain in 2022 by Simon & Schuster UK Ltd.
First US edition August 2022
SIMON & SCHUSTER BOOKS FOR YOUNG READERS
and related marks are trademarks of Simon & Schuster, Inc.
For information about special discounts for bulk purchases, please contact Simon & Schuster
Special Sales at 1-866-506-1949 or business@simonandschuster.com.
The Simon & Schuster Speakers Bureau can bring authors to your live event.
For more information or to book an event, contact the Simon & Schuster Speakers Bureau
at 1-866-248-3049 or visit our website at www.simonspeakers.com.
The text for this book was set in Museo Slab.
Manufactured in China
0122 SUK
2 4 6 8 10 9 7 5 3 1
Library of Congress Cataloging-in-Publication Data
Names: Small, Steve (Animator) author, illustrator.
Title: Wellington's big day out / Steve Small.
Description: First edition. | New York : Simon & Schuster Books for Young Readers, 2022. | "A Paula Wiseman
Book." | Audience: Ages 4–8. | Audience: Grades 2–3. | Summary: Wellington the elephant cannot wait to grow
up, but when he receives a jacket that is too big for him on his birthday, Wellington is worried he is too small.
Identifiers: LCCN 2021054212 (print) | LCCN 2021054213 (ebook) |
ISBN 9781665922555 (hardcover) | ISBN 9781665922562 (ebook)
Subjects: CYAC: Elephants—Fiction. | Growth—Fiction. | Size—Fiction.
Classification: LCC PZ7.1.S594335 We 2022 (print) | LCC PZ7.1.S594335 (ebook) | DDC [E]—dc23
LC record available at https://lccn.loc.gov/2021054212
LC ebook record available at https://lccn.loc.gov/2021054213

One Saturday morning, Wellington woke up early. *Today is going to be a good day*, he thought.

All Saturdays were good, but this Saturday was *even* better. It was Wellington's birthday. He was a whole year older than he was yesterday. . . .

I'm **definitely** *more grown up*, he thought.

He walked into the kitchen to see if his mom and dad would notice.

"Who is this gentleman?" said Mom. "What have you done with Wellington and why are you wearing his bathrobe?" said Dad.

"Why, it IS Wellington!" they said together. **"Happy birthday, Wellington!"**

Wellington was just enjoying his third pancake, when he noticed a present on the seat next to him.

He was very excited.
But now that he was
older, he gently picked
it up and opened it
carefully, the way his
mom and dad would
open their presents.

It was just what
he wanted.
A new jacket
exactly like Dad's.

It was perfect.

Except that it was too big.

Seeing the look of disappointment on Wellington's face, Mom said, "Why don't you two go and visit the tailor in the city while I make a cake? Dad gets his jackets fixed there. You can see Grandad, too."

Wellington thought this sounded like a very grown-up thing to do and nodded happily.

When Wellington told the bus driver
how old he was, the bus driver sighed.
"I'm afraid that means you'll have to start
paying for tickets now, Wellington."
"Really?" Wellington said with a big smile.

Dad bought their tickets and they both
took a seat.

BIG BIG

"I've never seen anyone so happy about having to pay for something," his dad said, chuckling.

Wellington looked at the ticket. *It's only half fare, but it's a start*, he thought to himself.

The city was very busy, and Wellington could hardly even see the sky through all the passersby. He asked his dad for a shoulder ride. "I thought everything looked big from the ground, but up here it's HUGE," Wellington said.

When they arrived at the tailor's, it was closed.
They decided to look around the music shop
next door while they waited for
it to open again.

Dad played a huge shiny tuba.

But when it was Wellington's turn,
and though he blew as hard as he could,
he could barely get it to make a sound. . . .

Wellington's dad was about to ask if he wanted
to try something smaller, when he spotted the
tailor walking by.

But when they got
outside, the tailor had gone.
This time they decided to wait
in the ice cream parlor.

Dad chose the Super-Size Strawberry Sundae.

So did Wellington.

It was very, very good. But as tasty as it was,
Wellington couldn't quite finish it.

"It's just too **big**!" he gasped,
his tummy as tight as a drum.

Back outside, they found the tailor
had, once again, come and gone.

They both sighed.

Wellington's dad looked at his watch.
"It's time we went to Grandad's,"
he said, and they jumped in a cab.

HUFF PUFF
     HUFF PUFF
          HUFF PUFF

Grandad lived just outside the city.
The house was always fun to visit because
Grandad rarely threw anything away.
There was so much to see.

"Happy birthday, Wellington!
My, how you've grown!" said Grandad.
Wellington smiled, but the smile didn't want to stay. . . .

"Wellington's new jacket is too big," said Dad.

"It's not too big," said Wellington,
letting out a long sigh.

"I'm just

too

small."

Grandad sat beside him for a moment.
"I was just the same when I was young,
Wellington. All I wished for was to
grow up as fast as I could.

"That's the trouble with wishes," he sighed.
"Sometimes they come true."

SIGH!

Grandad pulled some pencils from his pocket and said, "Wellington, would you mind standing against that wall, please?"

Wellington did so, and Grandad drew a line on the wall marking the top of his head.

Wellington turned and noticed another set of lines next to his. "What's that?" he asked.

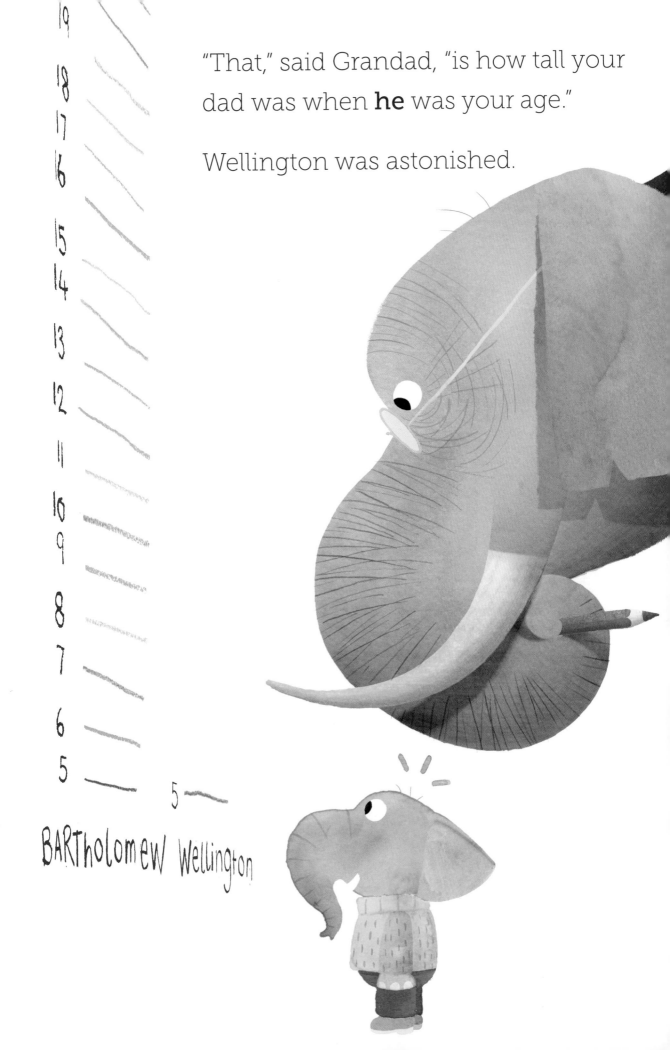

"That," said Grandad, "is how tall your dad was when **he** was your age."

Wellington was astonished.

19
18
17
16

15
14

13

12

11

10
9

8

7

6

5
5

BARTholomew Wellington

Grandad chuckled. "Yes," he said, "your dad was exactly the same height as you are now."

YAY   WOO WOO   YAY!

Wellington smiled
a very BIG smile.
And this time
it stayed there
for a while.

"Wellington?" said Grandad. "How would you like to go ice-skating this afternoon?"

"What if they don't have skates that fit me?" Wellington asked.

"Why, that's easy," said Grandad. "I want you to have the ones I used to wear when I was your age."

"I think we'll miss the tailor if we go skating," said Dad.

Wellington thought about it for a moment.
He looked at the lines on the wall.

Then he looked at the jacket . . .

and at the skates.

"Maybe the jacket will fit me better
next year," he said.

They had a wonderful time at the ice rink and stayed until the sun went down.

And the skates?

They fit perfectly.